ANIMALS DO WHAT?

ANIMALS IN THE AIR

By Brenda McHale

Published in 2023 by Enslow Publishing, LLC
29 East 21st Street, New York, NY 10010

© 2022 Booklife Publishing
This edition is published by arrangement with
Booklife Publishing

Edited by:
Emilie Dufresne

Designed by:
Dan Scase

All rights reserved. No part of this book may be reproduced in any form without permission in writing from the publisher, except by a reviewer.

Manufactured in the United States of America

CPSIA compliance information: Batch #CSENS23: For further information contact Enslow Publishing LLC, New York, New York at 1-800-398-2504.

Please visit our website, www.enslowpublishing.com.
For a free color catalog of all our high-quality books, call toll free 1-800-398-2504 or fax 1-877-980-4454.

Find us on

Cataloging-in-Publication Data

Names: McHale, Brenda.
Title: Animals in the air / Brenda McHale.
Description: New York : Enslow Publishing, 2023. I Series: Animals do what? I Includes glossary and index.
Identifiers: ISBN 9781978531307 (pbk.) I ISBN 9781978531321 (library bound) I ISBN 9781978531314 (6 pack) I ISBN 9781978531338 (ebook)
Subjects: LCSH: Animal flight--Juvenile literature. I Birds--Juvenile literature. I Insects--Juvenile literature.
Classification: LCC QP310.F5 M343 2023 I DDC 591.47'9--dc23

PHOTO CREDITS

All images are courtesy of Shutterstock.com. With thanks to Getty Images, Thinkstock Photo and iStockphoto. Front cover – Andre Marais. 1 – Andre Marais. 4&5 – Enrique Ramos, Independent birds, Elina Litovkina, ilikestudio. 6&7 – Alexey Seafarer, Agami Photo Agency, MZPHOTO.CZ. 8&9 – Mike Truchon, BobNoah, Sabrina Patrice, Ondrej Prosicky. 10&11 – Independent birds, Ethan Daniels, Nathapol Kongseang, Fabio Maffei. 12&13 – Seregam, Daniel Prudek. 14&15 – Marcos Amend, Martin Grossma 16&17 – ChameleonsEye, Nadiia Balytska. 18&19 – Eric Isselee, Travel Stock, Chris Humphries, David Havel. 20&21 – Subbotina Anna, enciktat, Keng Samukkheenitch. 22&2 – Lisa Strachan, Joshua Davenport, Ang Kean Leng, Agnieszka Bacal, Sinesp. Background on all pages – tanewpix789.

CONTENTS

PAGE 4	What Things Fly?
PAGE 6	Albatross
PAGE 8	Hummingbird
PAGE 10	Bat
PAGE 12	Bee
PAGE 14	Hoatzin
PAGE 16	Hercules Moth
PAGE 18	Vulture
PAGE 20	Dragonfly
PAGE 22	Does It Fly?
PAGE 24	Glossary and Index

Words that look like <u>this</u> can be found in the glossary on page 24.

WHAT THINGS FLY?

The air is not just for <u>birds</u>. There are quite a few creatures that fly and some of them do some strange things. Here are some types of animals you can find in the sky...

Birds such as toucans

Insects such as dragonflies

Mammals such as bats

BUTTERFLY

Type: Insect
Found: Worldwide (usually close to flowers)
Diet: Usually nectar from flowers

On each page you will see a fact file like this. It will give you cool facts about the animal, such as what type of animal it is, its diet, and its habitat.

ALBATROSS

ALBATROSS
Type: Bird
Found: Southern Ocean and North Pacific Ocean
Diet: Squid and fish

Wingspan

The albatross has the biggest wingspan of any bird. Some have a wingspan of over 10 feet (3 m). That's nearly as long as a car!

They can smell a tasty meal from 12.5 miles (20 km) away.

Scientists have been collecting albatross poop to find out how <u>climate change</u> is affecting what they eat.

Albatrosses can fly for hours without even flapping their wings. They ride the <u>air currents</u> like a hang glider.

Scientists believe that albatrosses might sleep while they fly.

They spend the first three to ten years away from land after they learn to fly.

An albatross can fly around the world in just 46 days!

HUMMINGBIRD

Hummingbirds can fly backward and hover like helicopters.

HUMMINGBIRD
Type: Bird
Found: North and South America
Diet: Insects and nectar

The bee hummingbird is the smallest bird in the world. It is about 2 inches (5 cm) long. That is not much longer than a child's thumb.

The bee hummingbird's eggs are the size of peas.

It can weigh as little as two grams. That is less than half a grape!

8

A hummingbird's wings flap 50 to 200 times every second. That's what makes the hum.

Its heart beats at more than 1,000 beats a minute. Ours beat at 60 to 100 beats a minute.

The sword-billed hummingbird's beak is longer than its body.

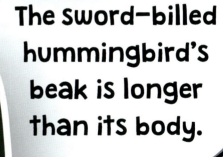

BAT

BAT

Type: Mammal
Found: Worldwide except very cold places
Diet: Insects, fruit, small animals, or blood depending on the type

Vampire bats drink other animals' blood.

They sneak up on them in the dark. They then bite them and suck their blood, just like a vampire!

Almost all types of bats rest hanging upside down.

Some bats can drop their body temperature very low when they hibernate.

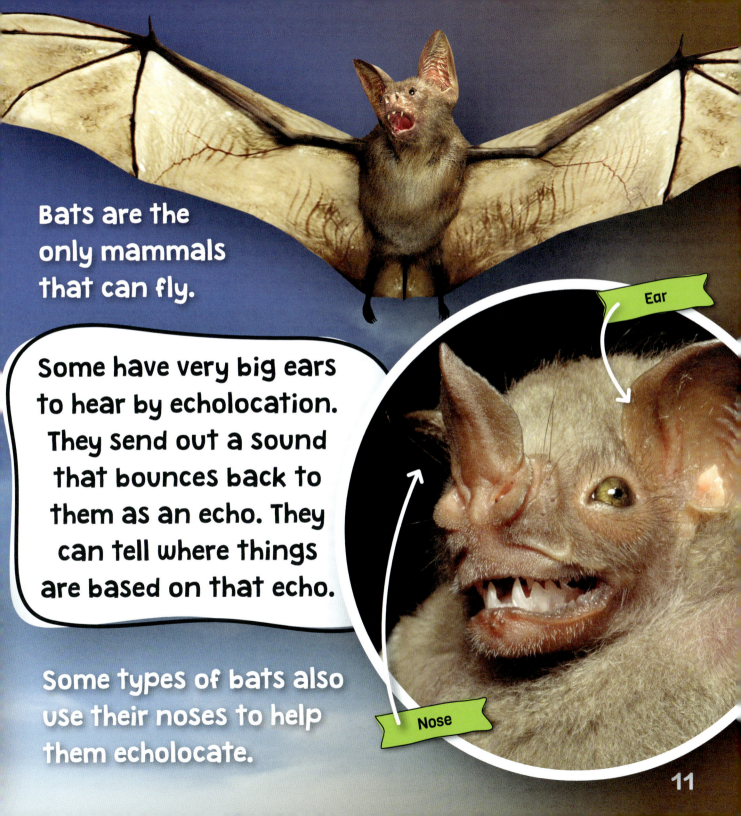

Bats are the only mammals that can fly.

Some have very big ears to hear by echolocation. They send out a sound that bounces back to them as an echo. They can tell where things are based on that echo.

Some types of bats also use their noses to help them echolocate.

Ear

Nose

BEE

A bee only makes about one-twelfth of a spoon of honey in its lifetime. That is not even enough for a cup of tea.

BEE
Type: Insect
Found: Worldwide except in very cold places
Diet: Mostly pollen

Bees dance and wiggle their bums to tell other bees in the hive the right direction to go for food.

A bee can recognize different human faces!

Bees all have their own jobs. Some guard and others find the nectar. Some keep the nest clean. There are even undertaker bees who take the dead bees out of the nest.

This bee's job is to collect pollen.

HOATZIN

The hoatzin smells so bad that some people call it the stinkbird.

HOATZIN
Type: Bird
Found: South America
Diet: Leaves, flowers, and fruit

The chicks have claws on their wings and use them to climb trees.

It only eats plants and has a stomach a bit like a cow to <u>digest</u> them.

It's not good at flying. Part of its digestive system is so big that it makes it harder for the hoatzin to fly.

HERCULES MOTH

Large wingspan

HERCULES MOTH
Type: Insect
Found: Australia and Papua New Guinea
Diet: Nothing!

Animals in the Air

The hercules moth is the biggest moth, with a wingspan of 10.5 inches (27 cm). Each wing is the size of an adult's hand.

It stays in a cocoon for up to two years.

A big moth grows from a big caterpillar. The hercules moth caterpillar is 4.7 inches (12 cm) long.

Hercules moth leaving cocoon

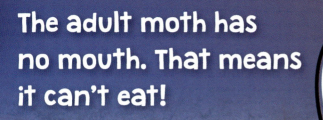

The adult moth has no mouth. That means it can't eat!

It usually only lives for between two days and two weeks, just long enough to <u>mate</u> and lay eggs.

Female hercules moths make a smell so strong that it can be smelled from 1.2 miles (2 km) away.

17

VULTURE

Most types of vultures have a bald head. That means when they dig their head into a dead animal to eat it, they stay cleaner.

VULTURE

Type: Bird
Found: Everywhere except Australia and Antarctica
Diet: Animals that are already dead

Vultures eat rotten meat that other animals can't eat.

Sometimes they eat so much that they can't get off the ground when they try to fly.

They sometimes pee and poop on their legs to cool down!

They have special stomachs that can kill <u>bacteria</u>. That's why they can eat rotten meat.

DRAGONFLY

DRAGONFLY
Type: Insect
Found: Near fresh water around the world
Diet: Smaller insects

Dragonflies from 300 million years ago had a wingspan of up to 1.6 feet (0.5 m)!

They snatch flying insects out of the air for food as they are flying. They catch them with their feet.

Dragonflies can fly at speeds of over 18 miles (29 km) per hour. That's faster than a speeding cyclist.

Males will fight to the death to keep other males away from their area.

Dragonflies can hover like helicopters. Scientists are trying to make a robot that moves in the same way.

DOES IT FLY?

There are lots of things that you might see in the air that can't actually fly.

A good wave of its fins will keep a flying fish out of the water for about 45 seconds. Then it falls back into the water to breathe.

Flying frogs use the skin between their fingers and toes to glide through the air.

Flying squirrels have their very own parachute in between their arms and legs.

These wing suits work just like the flying squirrel's skin.

GLOSSARY

air currents	movement of air
bacteria	tiny living things, too small to see, that can cause illness
birds	animals with feathers, two wings, and two feet
climate change	a change in the typical weather or temperature of a large area
diet	the kinds of foods that a person or animal usually eats
digest	to break down food into things that can be absorbed and used by the body
habitat	the natural home in which animals, plants, and other living things live
hibernate	to spend the winter sleeping or resting
insects	animals with one or two pairs of wings, six legs, and no backbone
mammals	animals that are warm-blooded, have a backbone, and produce milk to feed their children
mate	to produce young with an animal of the same species
nectar	a sweet liquid made by plants
pollen	yellow powder made by flowering plants

INDEX

blood 10
diets 5–6, 8, 10, 12, 14, 16, 18, 20
flowers 5, 14
hearts 9
helicopters 8, 21
nectar 5, 8, 13
oceans 6
water 20, 22
wings 7, 9, 14, 16, 23
wingspans 6, 16, 20